Justice

KYMBALI CRAIG

An imprint of Enslow Publishing

WEST 44 BOOKS™

**Please visit our website, www.west44books.com.
For a free color catalog of all our high-quality books,
call toll free 1-800-542-2595 or fax 1-877-542-2596.**

Cataloging-in-Publication Data

Names: Craig, Kymbali.
Title: Justice / Kymbali Craig.
Description: New York : West 44, 2020.
Identifiers: ISBN 9781538384220 (pbk.) | ISBN 9781538384237
 (library bound) | ISBN 9781538384244 (ebook)
Subjects: LCSH: Schools--Juvenile fiction. | Theft--Juvenile fiction. |
 Truthfulness and falsehood--Juvenile fiction.
Classification: LCC PZ7.C735 Ju 2020 | DDC [F]--dc23

First Edition

Published in 2020 by
Enslow Publishing LLC
101 West 23rd Street, Suite #240
New York, NY 10011

Design: Seth Hughes
Cover Art: Tyler D. Ballon

Printed in the United States of America

CPSIA compliance information: Batch #CS19W44: For further information contact
Enslow Publishing LLC, New York, New York at 1-800-542-2595.

This book is dedicated to the streets of Chicago, Illinois; Hattiesburg, Mississippi; and New York City, for they are the roads on the journey from which many of my stories began. To my dearest family and all the folks who supported me along the way.

CHAPTER 1

From the jump, the day seemed to be just a little off. First of all, Justice already knew he had to stay after school for a make-up test. It was for an English exam he flunked. Luckily, his mother didn't know anything about it. If she found out, she would be very disappointed. So Justice would do whatever he could to raise the failing grade without her finding out.

If that means staying after school to take a make-up test, so be it. It's no big deal. It's always nice to talk with Ms. Clarendon anyway, Justice thought. *She's been so supportive of my songwriting and my raps. I'd like to get her take on some new lyrics I've written. They're sort of all over the place. I'm not sure what direction I want the song to take. I'm not used to writing about...romantic stuff. I don't want to lose that edge, that swagger.*

Ms. Clarendon's English class was Justice's last period of the day. A lot of the students stayed after their lunch periods just to go to her class. She always encouraged everybody to do their best. She was the coolest teacher in school.

Plus, by staying late, I get to spend more time looking at Ebony. Justice felt a dreamy smile slide across his face.

Ebony was a new student at Lake Forrest High. *The most beautiful girl I've ever seen.*

His best friend Eric thought he was in love with her. *But what does that fool know?!*

Ebony's mother was Asian. From Japan. And her father was an African American music producer from the neighborhood. Ebony was quiet and kind of shy, but mad cool. Justice liked her style.

Ebony didn't look or dress like anyone else in school or in the neighborhood. She wore clothes that no one had ever seen in the stores. No one knew where she found them. And she combined different styles into a whole new look. Faded jeans with a crimson velvet smoking jacket. A kente cloth headscarf with a t-shirt printed with Japanese characters. Motorcycle boots and what looked like a cocktail dress from the 1950s, a jean jacket that had been around the block more than once draped on her shoulders. A little hat with a net veil perched on her head. She somehow managed to look both street and classy all at once.

Ebony was out of this world. There was no one else like her. Not even close.

Justice's romantic daydream was shattered by the sound of his mother's alarm-like holler. That was the other thing that felt off this morning. His mother. She sounded like she was bustling around like mad. Huffing and puffing and muttering under her breath. Slamming pots and pans. Tossing plates and utensils on the breakfast table with irritation. Barking out orders with an unusually loud and angry voice.

"Hurry up, Justice! Your breakfast is ready. Come on, you'll make me miss my bus."

"COMING!"

Justice groaned but quickly finished getting dressed. He checked his look in the mirror. Nodded in approval. Then he grabbed his book bag and headed for the kitchen.

"Let me guess, the usual," he muttered under his breath. There it was on the table: toast with jelly, a piece of fried bologna, a small cup of orange juice on the side, and a hard-boiled egg. Boiled eggs are what they always ate when there was no butter left to make scrambled eggs.

Look happy and be thankful and appreciative, he coached himself.

Justice didn't want his mom to feel bad. He knew she was doing the best she could to take care of them. After all, she worked two jobs to keep things going. And they were better off than most people who lived in this 'hood.

Justice began to eat and remembered to be grateful and appreciative.

"Mmm-mmm. Delicious. This is the stuff!"

His mother softened a bit. More like her usual self. "Thank you, baby. I love to see my young man eating. But between swallows, show me your homework."

It was the same thing every morning. Justice was prepared with his folders. He tried not to show any signs of nervousness. He didn't want his mom to find out that he had failed a test last week or that he was making it up after school today. To cover his anxiety, he got up from the breakfast table and went to the living room while his mother reviewed his homework. He would just cool his heels there for a moment until he was sure he could be cool and composed. His mother's purse was sitting on the couch. He would need a snack, some brain food, to eat just before the test this afternoon. Justice began rooting around in the purse, looking for a power bar or something.

"Why are you going through my bag, Justice? What do you think you're doing? Who gave you permission?" Justice's mother stood in the doorway, arms crossed. Her morning irritation had flared into all-out rage. Justice was shocked into stillness and silence. He froze with his hand in her purse.

"Ma, why are you so mad? I'm just looking for a power bar. What's the big deal? You've never…"

"You don't go ransacking my purse without asking me. You don't touch my purse. You don't touch anyone's purse. Got it? Do you hear me, Justice?"

Justice was stunned and completely confused. What had gotten into his mother? She was not being herself this morning. At all. Did she know about the failed test?

"Ma, what's wrong? What did I do?"

His mother's face was hard and stony. She was fuming. But suddenly, she exhaled and it all went loose. Her shoulders sagged. Her eyes filled with tears. She began to shake her head sadly. So sadly.

"Come back to the breakfast table, Justice. You need to finish eating. And we have to talk."

Once seated across from each other, Justice's mother swallowed hard and took a deep, shaking breath.

"Justice, you have to be more careful. Somebody else might take your actions to mean something other than what they are. And it could get you in trouble. Something bad could happen to you."

"I hear you, Ma, but don't worry about that. I know how to handle myself."

"I'm not worried about you. I'm worried about the world outside this apartment. Some of the people you might run into. You are a young black male, and it isn't easy out there. I know it's sad, but it's also true. You have to work twice as hard to stay out of trouble as everybody else does. Twice as hard to look like you *aren't* trouble."

"I got that Ma, but where are you going with this? You're not telling me anything I don't already know."

Justice's mother paused to collect her thoughts. To control her emotions. Justice finished up his breakfast, stayed seated, and waited for her to continue.

"Something happened Justice. To someone I know. Right here in this neighborhood. Just the other day."

His mother paused. Trying to calm herself and collect her thoughts.

"This nice white girl at my job at the clinic was telling me her son had a close call with the police."

"For real, Ma? A white boy had a close call with the police?! About what!?"

"Well, her son isn't white. She's married to a black man, so their son is biracial. He's about your age, maybe a little older. He's on the track team at his school. One day last week, he and his friends were running down the street, racing each other. When they tore around the corner, a police officer appeared out of nowhere. He pulled out his gun and ordered them to freeze, get their hands up in the air, and get on the ground, face down. He said something about suspected armed robbery."

Justice's mother paused. She swallowed. Took a deep breath. Her voice was a little shaky.

"They were roughed up a bit, slammed

against the patrol car. They were cuffed and arrested. Brought down to the station. They were thrown into a holding cell. With adults. Some pretty rough people. They spent the whole night in there, scared to death. Finally, after about eighteen hours, they were released. Turns out that three other boys had robbed a gas station around the corner from where they had been racing each other. Just another case of mistaken identity. The real thieves were caught later that night after knocking off another gas station on the other side of the neighborhood."

Another pause. Justice waited, silent. He knew now was not the time to interrupt. His mother's chin began to tremble a little. When she again spoke, her voice was shaking more. With emotion. With sadness or anger or both. Justice couldn't tell.

"But my friend's son could have gotten beat up by that cop. The cop could have planted a gun or drugs on him. He could have been shot and killed by the police. These things happen. Every day. You gotta be careful, Justice! You gotta know what you're doing, and you gotta watch how you act. Just walking around out there, living your life, acting normal, you are under suspicion. You can be arrested just for being black. Now, you know we got big plans for you. And, God knows, I don't know what I would do if something happened to you." She choked up and stopped talking.

Justice reached across the kitchen table. He squeezed her hand.

"I'll be careful, Ma. I'll be smart out there."

"You do that, young man."

She wiped the tears from her eyes.

"Now we have to hustle on out of here. We're officially late."

They dropped their dishes into the sink.

"Now, get that garbage ready to take out, and wash them dishes up for me quick. I'll be right back. I have to fix my makeup. Hurry up now and be ready to go when I get back. Make sure you got all your stuff. You know how forgetful you are sometimes."

When she returned, Justice was ready to go. They grabbed their bags and headed out.

Outside, the street was quiet. The dealers

and the addicts were still asleep. They walked to the end of the block. Usually they would go in different directions at the corner. Today, though, his mother wanted to walk with him to the bus stop.

Justice thought to himself, *I'm about to be 16 years old, and she is still trying to walk me to school.* Maybe it was because their neighborhood was no joke. It was one of the worst 'hoods in Wilsonburg. His boys were waiting for him at the corner deli down the block. He thought maybe she was still thinking about the talk they had.

"I'm good from here, Ma."

His mother looked at him with a wrinkled brow. Her eyes were a little watery. Was it the wind? Or something else?

She sighed. "Okay, baby. I know you got this. Just be smart. And careful." She pulled him into an unusually tight hug, then whispered in a choked voice, "I'll see you at home later today. Right?"

"Sure thing, Ma. I'm going to be fine, don't worry. It's a beautiful day. What could possibly go wrong?"

CHAPTER 2

Justice watched his mom turn the corner. Before she disappeared from sight, she threw one last worried glance back in his direction. Justice waved and smiled. Then he turned and ran to catch the light at the crosswalk. He just made it across before the light turned red and the cars in the cross street started speeding his way. Justice slowed his roll. He made sure to approach his boys at a casual, unhurried pace.

I can't be showing up in a sweat, all out of breath. Gotta be cool. Get my swagger on.

Everybody met up in front of the corner store before heading to school—especially the girls. And that's why Justice and his friends were *really* there. It wasn't for the fried egg sandwiches or candy bars. His best friend Eric tried to talk to all the girls. Eric didn't care how good-looking they were, as long as they were girls.

"I love the ladies," he always said. "And the ladies love me, sure enough. No lie."

Eric was convinced that he had the magic touch with "the ladies." He saw himself as a smooth operator. Someone who knew how to talk to women. How to impress and charm them. The truth was, all the girls in school found him funny and entertaining. But that was about it. They liked him a lot. Just not in That Way. He was more like a goofy kid brother. Fun to have around and joke with and gently make fun of. But not boyfriend material. Eric either had no idea that this was the case, or he chose not to see the reality. Either way, he acted as if he truly believed he was the center of all female attention.

"What I got going here may look easy from where you're standing, Justice," Eric would often half-joke, wiping his brow. "But these women are running me ragged. Do you have any idea how exhausting it is being this desirable? Count yourself lucky, my brother. Trust me, I would LOVE to not be such a hot commodity. But it's my cross to bear. You play the hand you're dealt."

Justice was just the opposite. He had no interest in flirting. He wouldn't even know how to do it if he wanted to. He didn't fall for girls easily or casually. He liked being friends with girls a lot. And then flirting with them just felt weird. Like a lie or a game. He wanted to save that special kind of attention for the day when he *really* liked someone. And, whether he admitted it to himself or not, that day had arrived. Justice's heart was set on Ebony.

She's just so fine. It almost hurts to look at her.

Eric was holding court. Flirting with all the girls. Cracking up the guys. He was such a friendly, happy person. One of the few dudes in school who was popular with both girls and guys. No one had a beef with him. He didn't get into it with other guys, even though he tried to be such a player with the ladies. There was no competition or jealousy.

I don't know how he pulls that off, Justice thought to himself. *I guess it's 'cause Eric is so sweet. He's so open. There's nothing fake or sneaky about him. You get what you see. He just wants everyone to have a good time. There's plenty of fun to go around, and he wants everyone to get their fair share. Plus, he's loyal as they come. A true friend. He takes that seriously. Friendship is the one thing that's no joke to him.*

Eric was joking and flirting, trying to involve everyone in the good time. The girls were standing a bit apart, rolling their eyes. Whispering amongst themselves. Giggling. Pretending to be bored and unamused. The other boys were trying to show off. They were trying to draw attention to themselves and away from Eric. Pushing and shoving each other. Shows of strength.

"Justice, my man!" Eric yelled joyfully when he saw his friend approaching the group. For a moment, Eric even forgot about the girls surrounding him. He peeled away from the circle and went to give Justice a big hug and draw him into the group. He knew Justice was a bit shy. A bit of a loner. But he wanted to always include him.

That's what I mean. Loyal, Justice remarked to himself.

"You're late today, my brother. What gives?" Eric asked.

"Just a little hassle with my mom. Nothing serious."

"I know what that's all about. My mom gives me the business all day, every day. She never gets off my back."

"Just imagine what a mess you'd be if she didn't!" Justice cracked.

The girls all smiled and laughed. They busted on Eric. Gave Justice shy glances.

"All right, all right! I see how it is," Eric complained. He tried to look hurt, but he was smiling ear-to-ear. He looked happy that Justice had gotten a big laugh. Eric always joked about how the girls all liked Justice. Liked how quiet and serious he was. How he only spoke when he really had something to say. How he kept himself a little apart.

"As usual, Justice wins just by showing up," one of the other guys muttered under his breath. The defeated guys began to move off toward school, in a shuffling, shoving mass.

"We better get going too, Eric. Big day today," Justice said. He was choosing to ignore the adoring looks he was getting from the girls. They, too, wandered off as a group, trying to act extra cool.

"Big day? Oh yeah. Your big make-up test. You ready this time?" Eric asked.

"Ready as I'll ever be."

"I bet you're ready to see Ebony, too, right?"

Justice punched Eric playfully on the shoulder. "Don't you ever shut up?"

They moved off together toward school, laughing happily.

CHAPTER 3

All through the school day, Justice had a tough time staying focused on his classes. All he could think about were the moments alone he would have with Ebony later in the day. They were in the same English class during last period. And they were both taking the make-up test after that class.

What should I say to her? Should I try to make a joke? Will she laugh? Eric always says my jokes are corny. But Eric isn't exactly a comic genius.

Justice was so distracted that he couldn't concentrate. The school day drifted by while he daydreamed about Ebony. Suddenly, he snapped out of it. He realized that he had just five minutes left before last period.

Last period was his favorite class of the day, and not just because Ebony was in it. English was taught by the coolest and most popular teacher in the whole school, Ms. Clarendon. She wasn't like the other teachers. She was different, real down to earth. She had grown up in Copenhagen, Sweden. She was more open and trusting with the students. And for a white woman, she knew all kind of things about jazz, gospel, soul, and R&B. When it came to hip-hop, though, Ms. Clarendon really knew her stuff. She was familiar with the whole history of rap music. She could probably school anybody on the sheer poetry of hip-hop lyrics and the hidden meanings of all their references. Ms. Clarendon made Justice feel like he could be anything he wanted to be.

"All you have to do is set your mind to it and put in the work," she often said. "As Thomas Edison said, 'Genius is one percent inspiration and ninety-nine percent perspiration.' Put in the sweat equity, Justice! You can't just call yourself an artist and wait for inspiration to strike. Art is all about sitting down every day and working, working, working. Whether you want to or not. Even if you're tired or bored or have no ideas. Sit down and don't get up until you've produced something, no matter how bad. It's a start. Something to build on."

Justice was lost in his thoughts, remembering Ms. Clarendon's advice to him about his songwriting. Suddenly, the bell rang. Final period would begin in five minutes. Justice put his headphones on and pumped his favorite hip-hop song. He rushed through the halls. He ran straight past Eric and some of his other friends who were standing around and talking before class. He wanted to be sure he got a seat near Ebony, and he wasn't going to wait for his homeboys to get their acts together.

"Yo, Justice!" Eric called. "You runnin' from the law?"

Justice flashed him a smile but didn't stop or even slow down.

When Justice entered the classroom, Ms.

Clarendon was writing something on the blackboard. Her back was turned to him. Her purse with all of her belongings was sitting on her desk. Attempting to get her attention, Justice began reciting lyrics from the song he was listening to. It was a song by his favorite rap artists, Street Stealer and Bling Money.

"We get 'em. We gets it. We got it," Justice rapped. "I got yo bag in my pocket, yo money in my wallet. Yep! It's yo clothes that I'm rockin'. Turn around, drop yo head, turn yo back, and I got it. Yep! It's yo boy Street Stealer, it's yo boy Street Stealer."

This immediately got Ms. Clarendon's attention. As much as she liked hip-hop, she didn't like songs that promoted violence and illegal activities. She felt hip-hop music should inspire or enlighten you in some way. Like the old school rap songs did back in the day.

"Hey Justice, come on now, what's up with that? You know I'm not a big fan of that kind of lyric."

Justice removed his headphones but left them hanging around his neck for easy access.

21

"I get you, Ms. C, but these are my boys. Plus you gotta admit the beat is sick."

She finished writing the class assignment on the board. She then put the chalk back in her desk drawer.

"Yeah, I can hear that. OK, the beat is good. The drum patterns are pretty cool. But the lyrics are just completely ridiculous. Irresponsible. There are way better lyricists out there, and they have great beats too."

Ms. Clarendon knew her stuff, so there was no winning this argument. But Justice enjoyed debating her anyway. While they were discussing the content of hip-hop lyrics, other students had filled the classroom. After all that, Justice missed his opportunity to find a seat near Ebony. But he would have another chance to get closer to her during the makeup test. So he took a seat in the front row. It was the only seat available, but he didn't mind it much. He learned more that way. Whenever he sat in the back of the class with his friends, he had to admit he was always a little distracted by their joking around. But he enjoyed Ms. C's class, so he would eventually tune them out.

"Alright Ms. C, I see your point. But the reason I rapped you those lyrics—your bag is just sitting out in the open on your desk. Wide open, with all your stuff in there. But you're careful to put the chalk safely away in the desk drawer. Why don't you just hide your bag in there too?"

"It's not wide open, OK? It's just on my desk slightly opened. Sometimes I need to use my phone to find reference materials I might want to introduce you guys to. I also trust that you guys will respect my things just as much as I respect yours."

By this time the whole class was listening to their conversation. Justice was caught off guard with her response.

"Trust? You trust all of us? Are you for real, Ms. C?"

"Yes, Justice, I am 'for real.' I'm very serious. Look, when I was in college, we had what we called the Honor System. Most of the students left their dorm room doors unlocked during the daytime."

The entire class gasped.

"And yes, OK, there were some thefts over the four years I went there, but not nearly as many as you might expect. It also made us feel more like a community, because everyone respected each other's space, whether they knew one another or not. And there were thousands of students. It was quite an amazing experience. It really opened my mind to some things. If you show people trust, they will almost always prove themselves to be trustworthy. So, I thought to myself, well, why not see if we can try this system here in the classroom."

Now Justice liked Ms. Clarendon even more. He had never met someone—especially a teacher or authority figure—who was so respectful and trusting of others. But based on his experience, he still had doubts. He didn't think her idea would work here. And he didn't want to see her become a victim of theft.

"Miss C, no offense, but you're dreaming."

She smiled and raised her right fist in the air.

"Well, Martin Luther King was only one man. But he had a dream, and look what happened."

Eric found his opening and chimed in. "Yeah, well, I have a dream too. I'm dreaming that I got an Xbox 360 and the oh-so-fine Beyoncé is sitting here next to me right now." He stopped and looked around the room. "And I'm still dreaming." The entire class busted out laughing.

Once they settled down and got serious and the class really got underway, the period went by quickly. The only thing about sitting in the front row was that Justice would have to turn around in his seat to look at Ebony. He couldn't stare at her without anyone noticing.

As soon as the bell rang, Justice moved to the back of the class for the make-up test. Here, he would be sitting closer to Ebony. He was a pretty smart kid. Plus, he had really studied the material this time around. It was about the meaning of literary terms like simile, metaphor, personification, allegory, and symbolism. They also had to provide examples of each term, using their own writing. In studying for the test, Justice came to realize that he was already using all these techniques in his lyrics. His raps were literature!

Look out Shakespeare, I'm coming up on you! Justice thought to himself, smiling.

Being so well prepared, Justice breezed through the make-up test pretty quickly. He noticed Ebony was struggling. He was tempted to help her. He liked her an awful lot, but he couldn't risk the chance of being caught helping her cheat. He would already be in hot water if his mom found out about the make-up test itself. If he were also caught cheating, he'd be in the biggest trouble of his life. Justice flashed back to his mother's sudden and surprising anger this morning at breakfast. He kept his eye on his own paper and avoided even the briefest glance in Ebony's direction.

Ms. Clarendon was in the back of the classroom helping the other students when Ebony suddenly got up from her seat. She went to Ms. C's desk to sharpen her pencil. She looked over at Ms. C's bag with a strange look on her face. Justice saw this but didn't make much of it. He thought maybe it was because she was having a hard time with the test.

Justice tried to prolong the process of taking the test as long as he could. He was hoping to leave at the same time as Ebony. Maybe strike up a conversation. See if she wanted to get a coffee or a soda sometime after school. But she seemed to be a long way from finishing. He couldn't wait around any longer. He was going to be late for a game of chess in the park near his house. He played with an old man who hung out in the park most days. Mr. Womack played anyone who was willing and able. Justice had seen him around since he was a little kid. A year or so ago, he finally got the courage to ask the old man to teach him how to play.

"You never played before?" Mr. Womack had asked.

Justice shyly shook his head no.

"That's alright. Gotta start somewhere, some day. Have you played checkers?"

Justice nodded his head happily. He was

excited to be able to say he knew how to do something.

"You've got a foundation to build on then. Wanna start now?"

And so they started that very afternoon. One year later, Justice still hadn't ever beaten Mr. Womack. But he was getting closer. Every game, he was a little stronger and smarter. It wouldn't be much longer. He could feel it.

Justice got up and tried his best to walk past Ebony with all the swag he had. He hoped she was looking. Ms. Clarendon was still in the back helping the other students, so he dropped his test on her desk.

"Alright, peace out, Ms. C!"

Then he got up the nerve to say, "Later, Ebony." She smiled and replied, "Later, Justice." He couldn't believe she said his name. It sounded so soft and sweet when she said it.

Justice left the room with the biggest grin on his face. He was so distracted he had forgotten his hat.

"Shoot! Now I'm really going to be late."

Justice turned and went back to the classroom. As he stood on the threshold, about to open the classroom door, what he saw through the window made him freeze in place. His jaw dropped. His skin prickled. He could feel his heart pounding and his temples pulsing. He was not seeing this. This couldn't be real. There must be some explanation. It couldn't be what it looked like.

Because what it looked like was bad. What it looked like was unbelievable. What it looked like was Ebony stealing something from Ms. C's purse.

CHAPTER 4

Ebony, a thief? It's not possible. It doesn't make any sense. There must be some good explanation for what I saw. Or what I think I saw.

In a daze, Justice ran down the hall to the gym, where the after-school programs were held. Eric took part in the programs every afternoon. He wanted to tell Eric what he'd just seen. He wanted his best friend's perspective on it. He wanted Eric to tell him he was just bugging out. Ebony was no thief. She must have been pulling a prank. Or getting something Ms. C had asked for. Eric would calm him down and get him thinking straight.

But Eric was standing at the entrance to

the gym, by the locker room doors. He was surrounded by a group of their friends. He was in the middle of the group, laughing and joking and enjoying being the center of attention. Now was not the time to speak to Eric.

Plus, Eric has a big mouth. If I tell him, the rest of the school will know by dinnertime. The whole world will know. No one can know this. Not until I can speak to Ebony and hear what she has to say.

Justice turned and walked away from the gym.

Should I tell Ms. C what I think I saw? But I don't know exactly what I saw, and I don't want Ebony to get in trouble. Especially if I didn't really see what I think I saw. People will say I'm a snitch.

Nobody wanted to be labeled a snitch. Even if telling someone what you saw was the right thing to do. It all depended on who you told, and what you told, and who you told on. In the 'hood, if you got it wrong, it could mean the difference between life and death.

My life and death.

Justice walked down the hallway. He'd

leave the school building and go to the park. Play his regular chess game with Mr. Womack. He walked out the main doors and ran down the stairs leading to the street. He headed left toward the park. But Justice couldn't stop thinking about Ebony.

Ebony is a thief? The nicest, prettiest, sweetest girl in the entire school? Why would she do it? Didn't she hear what Ms. C had just said about the honor code? It's impossible. There has to be a good explanation.

Justice had to know what that explanation was. He came to a dead stop. He spun around. He headed back to school. Back up the stairs. Back into the building.

Like Eric, Ebony usually participated in the after-school activities in the gym. So Justice again walked down the hallway to the gym entrance. Eric and his crew had disappeared.

Thank goodness. Luck may be on my side.

Justice entered the gym and looked around. He saw Ebony sitting high up in the bleachers, on the far end of the basketball court.

If I approach Ebony just the right way, maybe I can convince her to put Ms. C's things back. Before she even notices they're gone.

Justice walked around the edge of the basketball court. The court was crowded with activity. Some guys were playing half-court basketball. Some girls were playing five-on-five on the other half of the court. Another group of girls was rehearsing cheerleading. Their routines were backed by the music of a small corps of drummers and horn players from the marching band. They were playing a march version of one of Justice's favorite hip-hop songs.

Dang, those guys are tight. It would be awesome to join forces with them. Maybe freestyle rap over their crazy drumline sound. That could be mad cool. But I've got to stay focused. I have more important things to do right now.

Ebony was sitting at an angle. Sort of sideways. Away from most of what was happening in the gym below. Justice climbed the bleachers and approached Ebony. She did not see him coming. As he drew nearer to Ebony, he saw that she had a cellphone. She was checking out profiles on Facebook and watching music videos. He had never seen her with a cellphone before. And certainly not one that nice. He thought it was possible that it was Ms. C's. Maybe this was what he had seen her take out of Ms. C's bag.

Ebony was quietly singing along to the music on the phone. She was so caught up in it that she didn't notice Justice was now standing right next to her. He stood there quietly and listened. It was so beautiful. She was singing low, almost under her breath. But Justice could still tell that she had a powerful voice, even better than some he heard on the radio.

"Wow, you sound amazing!"

The sound of his voice startled Ebony. She wasn't aware Justice had been standing there listening to her sing the entire song. She stopped singing immediately and hastily turned off the phone. She shoved it clumsily into the back pocket of her jeans. Almost as if she were trying to hide it.

"Hey Justice. Um…were you standing there this whole time?"

"Yes. I'm sorry to startle you but…your voice! It's incredible!"

Ebony blushed with embarrassed pleasure.

"No, it's not. But…thanks. Um…what are you doing here? I thought you left already."

Justice opened his mouth. He had no idea what would come out. He didn't choose his words carefully. He had no plan. Words just came tumbling out. Words that needed to be said. No matter what the consequences.

"I'm just gonna say it. I saw what you did. Or I think I saw what you did. I don't think that's your phone. I saw you take something outta Ms. C's bag. And I think you should just put it back. I'll help you. If we put it back now, she may never realize it was gone. She'll never know. And we can just forget the whole thing."

Ebony blushed with embarrassment again. But this was a different kind of blush. A different kind of embarrassment. It was more like shame. She couldn't look Justice in the eyes anymore. She looked down at the ground and folded her arms defensively.

"I'm kind of into the honor code Ms. C is trying to create," Justice continued. "Even though I think it's probably impossible. It's pretty cool, you know? She's trying to help us out. She's trusting us. She's respecting us. How many adults—how many white folks—have ever done that? We should respect Ms. C in return."

Justice turned to walk away. Then he stopped and turned back around. He gathered the courage to say one last thing.

"And I think you're kind of cool too. Really, really cool, actually. So would you PLEASE put back whatever you took? I would hate to have to see you as someone other than the coolest, most amazing person I will ever be lucky enough to know."

Now it was Justice's turn to blush deeply.

Whoa! I just said way too much. I need to get out of here. I think I might throw up.

Justice tried to look calm, cool, and collected as he retreated down the bleachers. He put his headphones back on and began rapping out loud the words to the song he was listening to. He thought he had a good flow and sounded almost exactly like the rapper on the song. He hoped Ebony was listening. Maybe *she* would be impressed with *his* voice.

Justice left the gym and headed back down the hallway towards the main entrance. Down the hall, he spotted Mr. Hencken, the school's head security guard.

Just my luck. What is with this day I'm having?!

This guy acted more like a corrections officer than the head of security. He treated the students more like criminals and inmates than kids to be safeguarded and protected.

Justice was just about to duck around a corner and avoid him when Mr. Hencken turned his head at the last second and noticed him.

"Stop right there, young man!" he barked, more like an army sergeant or police captain than the Rent-a-Cop he was. "Take those headphones off. Turn that music down. And explain to me why you are on these premises. Where do you belong right now? You are not part of the after-school programs. You are not allowed to walk around this building, roaming the halls, going wherever you wanna go, doing whatever you wanna do."

"Yeah, OK. Whatever, man," Justice responded rudely. He was never this rude to adults. But after this day, to run up against this guy...

"I'm not roaming the halls," Justice insisted. "I was taking care of some business. Helping a friend with something. And now I'm about to leave. Relax, I'm out of here."

Justice put his headphones back on and cranked up the volume. He drowned out the outraged response of Mr. Hencken. Justice hurried down the side hall to keep well ahead of him. But just as he was going down the back stairs toward the side exit doors, he saw Ms. Clarendon coming out of the staff bathroom.

You've got to be kidding me! This is getting ridiculous.

Justice tried to make it out the door before she noticed him. But he was unsuccessful. Naturally.

Just as his hand reached the door handle, Ms. C called out, "Hey Justice, what's up?

How did it go with the make-up test? Do you think you nailed it this time around?"

"Um...hey...what's up, Ms. C? Um... yeah...I studied for it this time, so...um...I think I aced it."

Justice felt a new awkwardness around Ms. C. His words didn't flow. He tripped over them. There was no energy in his voice. No spark in his conversation.

"That's great, Justice. Is everything alright?" Ms. C looked at him with a curious expression on her face. She must have been a little confused by his new shyness or coolness.

"Aw yeah, everything is fine, Ms. C. I'm just a little tired. After the test."

"Well, I won't keep you. Get home and rest and have a great...Wait a minute! I thought I saw you leave school earlier. Why are you still here?"

"Um...yeah...I just...you know...uh... stopped by the gym for a second."

"Oh, cool. Are you taking advantage of the after-school programs?"

Justice felt really bad lying to Ms. C, so he kept his reply a little fuzzy.

"Yeah, something like that. Good night, Ms. C."

"Good night, Justice. Rest up. See you tomorrow!"

That night, Justice didn't get very much sleep. He tossed and turned for hours. He lay in bed, eyes open, staring at the ceiling, until the early morning sun peaked through his window and began brightening his room.

Another day. What will this one bring? For Ebony? For me? For the both of us?

What am I going to do? What am I going to do?

CHAPTER 5

When Justice's mom entered his bedroom with her usual "Rise and shine!" greeting, he was already up and dressed.

"Well, it looks like somebody got some good sleep last night and is ready to go," his mother said. She was not even trying to hide her shock and surprise.

"You got that right, Ma," Justice replied. "No time for breakfast today, though. I have to get to school early for a study group. We're getting ready for the midterm exams."

"Alright baby, alright. You sure? You'll need some brain food." His mother was always worried he wouldn't eat enough.

"I'll be fine. I'll get a banana or something at the corner store."

"Well, take a dollar or two from my purse on your way out, baby."

Justice froze as he was walking past her out of his bedroom into the living room. He briefly looked her in the eye, then slid his gaze to the floor.

"You sure? You want me to go into your purse? Yesterday morning you..."

"Yesterday morning I overreacted. I was unfair to you. You know right from wrong. I shouldn't have been lecturing you. Yelling at you. I just get so scared for you...out there. Not everyone knows like I do what a great kid you are. Not a kid. A great young man."

Justice glanced up at his mother. Then looked down again. He smiled sadly.

"Thanks Ma. I...I love you." He gave her a quick hug, grabbed his backpack off the couch, and hurried to the apartment door. Before the tears in his eyes would begin to trickle down his cheeks. Before his strange sense of guilt would catch up to him, would make him say more to his mother than he wanted to. About yesterday.

But why do I feel guilty? I didn't do anything wrong! Could I have done anything differently? Should I have? If Ebony doesn't make this right today, what should I do?

These questions dogged Justice all the way to school. And no good answers presented themselves.

Justice had skipped breakfast, and now he also skipped hanging out with his friends before school. He took the long way to school, on different streets. He wanted to avoid meeting up with everyone outside the corner store. He had only one thing on his mind. And he didn't feel like talking about it.

I don't want to see Eric. He'll sense something's wrong with me. He'll somehow get the secret out of me. Then it won't be a secret anymore. Everyone will know. Until Ebony and I figure out a way to deal with this, no one else can know.

Justice got to school and got in line for the metal detectors and bag search.

Thank goodness Mr. Hencken isn't man-

ning the station this morning. I don't need that hassle on top of everything else.

As soon as he got through the security station, Justice began looking for Ebony. No luck. The first period bell rang. Justice had no choice but to dash off down the hall and get to class. He took a seat in the back of the room. He usually sat toward the front. He liked to be able to see the blackboard clearly. And he liked the teacher being able to see him when he raised his hand. It was easier to join in the class discussions and get your questions answered when you sat closer to the teacher.

I just want to hide back here today. I can't think about anything but Ebony and her situation right now.

Justice spent the entire class period gazing out the window, thinking. And thinking some more. He spent all the morning's classes this way. Between classes, he scanned the hallways for Ebony but never saw her.

When the lunch bell rang, Justice ran out of his classroom. He was moving so fast that he almost knocked over Shaun, a classmate, on the way to the cafeteria.

"What the…?! Yo, Justice! Watch out!"

"Sorry, man. My bad."

Justice tried to be one of the first students to get to the cafeteria so he could see everyone who entered. But she wasn't there either. And she didn't show up by the end of lunch period.

The next couple of classes after lunch were brutal.

Still no Ebony. Where is she? Is she OK? Is she sick? Is she afraid that I snitched? Did she confess and get suspended? Or even expelled? Was she arrested?!

Justice's mind was working overtime. It was going to dark places. Leaping to the worst conclusions.

Stay cool, Justice. Calm down. It's probably nothing. Everything is fine. Probably. Everything is going to get smoothed out. Just stay calm and be patient. Don't freak out and do anything stupid or hasty.

Finally the sixth period bell rang. It was time for English class and Ms. C…and Ebony. When Justice entered the classroom, it was quieter than usual. Something immediately felt off. The atmosphere was heavy. A little sad. A little angry.

Ms. C wasn't as upbeat and lively as usual. She looked sort of blank. A little stony. Justice went to take a seat in the back near his friends.

I don't feel comfortable sitting up front with all that is going on and before I get a chance to talk to Ebony. I should keep a safe distance from Ms. C. Just until Ebony and I can figure out how to get Ms. C's stuff back where it belongs.

Ms. C's voice cut through Justice's thoughts.

"Alright, guys. Let's settle down. Everybody take a seat."

Sensing that something serious was up, everyone took their seat and quieted down more quickly than usual.

"I want to talk to you guys about something. Something important."

Justice froze in his seat. He knew this was the moment she would reveal to the class that she had been robbed.

"Um…OK…I'll get right to the point. Yesterday some things were taken from my bag. And…um…it had to have happened somewhere between sixth period and after-school activities. So if any of you guys know anything about it or maybe if it was one of you, it's OK. You can come talk to me about it. I won't be upset or anything like that. No one will get in trouble. It will just be between us. I know we all make mistakes sometimes and I know we're all on the same team here. So don't let me down. I just need my things back, OK?"

Was she looking right at me when she said that last part?! Justice asked himself. *I'm almost positive she did. Does she think I did it?!*

This made Justice nervous. He started to sweat a little.

Does she suspect that I know something about this? How could she suspect? She's pretty sharp. Maybe she figured it out. But I'm not going to say anything to her. Not until I talk to Ebony first.

Then Eric piped up.

"Aw man, somebody robbed you already, Ms. C? That's cold! I was kinda feeling that honor system thing you were trying out. Woulda been cool if that could work. But I told you, you were dreaming."

"Shut up Eric!" Justice growled, a little too loudly.

Eric looked at Justice, startled and hurt.

"What's up with you, Justice?"

"OK, everybody. Let's just settle down," Ms. C ordered. "Let's turn our attention toward today's writing exercise."

Eric turned again to Justice while Ms. C was writing on the blackboard and her back was turned to the class.

"You alright? You look like you seen a ghost or something. You're not the thief, so why are you bugging out?"

"I'm not bugging out. I'm just saying let's not make a big deal out of it. It'll just make it worse."

"Yeah, alright, alright. But who do you think did it?"

Justice shrugged but didn't respond. He sat in a daze for the remainder of the class. His mind was on Ebony. He would go look for her after school. Maybe he would find her somewhere in the 'hood.

Finally the bell rang, but Justice was so caught up in his thoughts that he hadn't noticed. Eric had to snap him out of it.

"Yo, come on Mr. Deep Thoughts. It's time to go."

Justice began to gather his things and got up to go.

"Justice! May I talk to you for a moment? In private?" Ms. C stood beside her desk with her hands on her hips. She looked unusually stern.

Oh, boy. This looks bad. This looks like trouble.

CHAPTER 6

Ms. Clarendon looked mad. A little sad too. But mostly just plain mad. Justice had never seen that expression on her face before.

"What's that all about?" Eric whispered. "I'm outta here. Catch up with me later and let me know what she wants."

Justice slumped back down in his seat. All the other students had left the classroom leaving just him and Ms. C.

"Take a seat up here near me, Justice." She was growing even sterner. She looked and sounded like a stranger all of a sudden. The odd new look on her face sparked his curiosity, so Justice looked her directly in the eye.

But because of what he knew, he grew uncomfortable. He looked down at his shoes.

"Look, Justice. I have to admit, I'm little disappointed about all of this. I mean I expected so much more from you."

She does think I did it! She thinks I'm the thief! How could she?!

Justice raised his head in shock. Searched her face for the old Ms. C. The one who liked and admired and trusted him.

"Don't worry, I'm not going to write up a report, OK? I don't want to make a big deal about this. I just need you to return my cellphone and my wallet. And I need it back on my desk by tomorrow morning. Then we can put this whole thing behind us and start over with a clean slate. OK? How's that?"

Justice stood up, unsteady on his feet. He was shocked. He couldn't believe she thought he was the thief. His feelings were hurt. He was insulted. He was offended.

It turns out she doesn't know me at all. After all this time. After all our conversations.

He respected Ms. Clarendon a lot. After all, he was the one who tried to warn her about the dangers of the honor code before she got robbed. And he had spent the last 24 hours trying to get her things back. By doing so, he was risking whatever romantic chance he had with Ebony. Risking being labeled a snitch in school and in the 'hood. And now Ms. C was accusing him of being the thief!

"No disrespect, but are you for real, Ms. C? What are you trying to say? That I'm a thief? You think I stole your stuff?"

"OK, relax, Justice. Just calm down. Sit back down. There's no one in here but you and me, so you can say whatever you need to."

"I am saying what I need to, Ms. C. It wasn't me. I didn't do it. Do we have anything else to discuss?"

"Oh, come on, Justice. I mean, you practically threatened me with those ridiculous rap lyrics you recited yesterday. And Mr. Hencken said he saw you roaming the halls after school. I ran into you myself in the hallway after school, skulking around the side exit. Looking pretty sneaky and sketchy. So I thought that maybe we could handle this ourselves. But only if you can be honest with me and admit what you did."

Justice just sat there, stunned. He looked at Ms. Clarendon with disbelief.

She thinks SHE feels disappointed? I can't believe this is the same woman I admired just yesterday.

Justice thought about the conversation he had with his mother yesterday morning. This was the moment it finally hit him.

This is exactly what Ma tried to warn me about. About what it means to be a young black man. How no one trusts you. Gives you the benefit of the doubt. No one really sees you. They only see a suspect, a criminal, a convict. Even someone who claims to be "woke." Someone "cool" like Ms. C.

"Hey, look, Justice, if you don't want to talk about this and you're going to have such a bad attitude about it, then I'll just have to make an official report. If I don't get my things back by tomorrow morning, I will request your suspension. I promise you that I don't want to have to do that."

Justice stared at her. A hard and direct

and unblinking stare. Lasting several seconds. Then he shook his head and sighed deeply.

What's that expression? "More in sorrow than in anger."

Justice stood up slowly. His body felt slow and heavy and tired. Sad. He walked toward the classroom door. When he was about to open it to leave, he turned back to her.

"I told you I didn't do it, Ms. Clarendon. That should be enough for you. If I say something, I mean it. It is true."

Justice put on his headphones and left the room. Now he was definitely on the hunt for Ebony. He couldn't get suspended for something he didn't do.

Justice looked everywhere for her. First, he went to the deli around the corner from school. A lot of students hung out there after school. But there was no sign of Ebony. So he went to the playground inside the housing project a couple of blocks down the street. It wasn't really a playground for little kids anymore, unfortunately. It had been taken over by gangbangers. They hung out there. Lots of people flowed through the housing proj-

ect's courtyard. Some just going about their business. Coming home from work. Bringing home groceries. Sitting on park benches and shooting the breeze. Others came to buy drugs dealt by the gang members.

He didn't think it was likely that Ebony would be here. But he had just found out she was a thief. So maybe he didn't know her as well as he thought he did. He had to cover all the bases. But she wasn't there either. Thank God.

Justice got out of there before any of the gang members zeroed in on him and called him over.

I don't need to be shaken down or recruited. This day is going badly enough already.

Next Justice headed over to the Boys and Girls Club. This was a popular after-school hangout for kids who didn't feel like dodging either Mr. Hencken or the gangbangers. It was a safe place to shoot hoops, take art or computer classes, plan for careers, and just have fun, talking and joking with friends and other kids from the neighborhood. At the entranceway, Justice spotted Eric, once again

in the middle of a circle of friends. Holding court, a captive audience.

Why is Eric always blocking the entrances of places? Always in the center of the action? The loudest voice in a gang of loud voices?

For a moment, Justice resented Eric. He was everywhere. He showed up whenever Justice most wanted to avoid him. Wanted to talk his ear off when Justice only wanted to get away, to keep silent. But watching Eric in action, in his element, Justice couldn't help but grin.

The guy is magnetic. He just loves people. Loves talking to people. How can you not love him for that?

At the moment, Eric was freestyling a rap. He was busting on everyone standing around him while pumping himself up. Classic Eric. And his audience loved it, even the put-downs about themselves!

Justice tried to walk on by without Eric spotting him. But as he was almost past the stairs in front of the club entrance, Eric sang out.

"Hey, bro! Come over here. I need you to

show these knuckleheads how to flow like a real pro. Come on, man. Come blaze the mic for me, bro."

Justice reluctantly walked over to the group.

"What's up? How you doing? Good to see y'all," Justice greeted the whole crew. "I can't hang out right now, Eric. I gotta handle something. Peace, y'all. Later."

He walked away with a wave.

"Hold tight, y'all. No rapping till I get back. Give me a second," Eric told his friends. He jogged to catch up to Justice.

"Hold up for a sec, yo. So what gives? I saw you talking to Ebony yesterday afternoon on the bleachers. My boy, you finally got up the nerve to step to her, huh? What did she say?"

Although Eric had a big mouth, Justice had never kept a secret from him. Until now.

"It was nothing, man," Justice replied.

"Yeah, right. It didn't look like nothing. From what I saw, it looked like you were in La La Land."

They both laughed.

"Whatever, man. You trippin'. I gotta go, Eric. I'll talk to you about it later."

Justice hurried off and walked over to the park. Some of the girls jumped double Dutch on the handball courts or sometimes they hung out down by the jungle gym. But Ebony wasn't there. He went a couple blocks over to the basketball courts. Sometimes the girls went there to cheer the boys on and catch their eye. Deep down, he'd hoped Ebony wasn't one of them and he wouldn't find her there. He didn't. But he did run into one of her friends. She said Ebony had left a few minutes before he arrived. Now he was starting to get anxious. After all, if he didn't find Ebony, there was a strong possibility he would be suspended. He couldn't let that happen. His mother would be furious. He searched everywhere he could think. But Justice didn't find Ebony anywhere. She had vanished.

Finally, as the sun began to sink and it grew dark, Justice went home.

I better get home before Ma. I need time to think. Figure out a plan. What I'm going to do.

When he entered the apartment, however, he saw his mother's purse on the dining table. He heard her voice. She was on her cell phone. She wasn't doing much of the talking. But when she did, her voice was weird. Sort of small and strained. Almost strangled in her throat. He heard her say, "Yes, thank you for letting me know. I am very sorry about all of this. Yes, we will see you tomorrow. Both of us. Goodbye."

Then Justice heard her voice again. Coming from the kitchen. Loud and clear. Not small and strained and strangled anymore. Big and powerful and angry.

"JUSTICE! COME IN HERE RIGHT NOW!"

CHAPTER 7

Uh-oh. This isn't good. She's got that mad voice again. But, like, it's crazy-mad this time.

"DID YOU NOT HEAR ME?! I SAID COME HERE RIGHT NOW!"

Justice walked toward the kitchen. He felt like a condemned prisoner. Dead man walking. After what felt like an hour, he finally entered the kitchen. Full of dread, he dared a look at his mother's face. Big mistake. She looked terrifying. He'd never seen this expression before. She stared at him, fuming. Didn't say anything for a long time. Too long. Justice was squirming under her fierce gaze. Finally she opened her mouth to speak.

"Sit down," she barked.

Dinner was already on the table. Fried chicken with rice and gravy. One of Justice's favorite meals. He had no need to pretend he liked this meal, unlike breakfast. This was the good stuff. She must have been making it before the phone call she had just finished. Who had been on the other line? Was it someone from school? Ms. Clarendon?

Justice and his mom sat for a moment, eating in a painful and tense silence. Neither of them was tasting the food. They just chewed and swallowed, without any pleasure.

Maybe I should try to crack a joke. Break the ice.

He tried a compliment instead.

"Delicious as always, Mom."

If Justice hoped this would soften her, he was wrong. She didn't respond. She didn't even seem to hear him. Justice went back to chewing and swallowing. This was misery.

Finally, his mom stopped eating and put her fork down. She breathed a huge sigh that was both angry and weary. And a little frightened. She put her elbows on the table. His mother never put her elbows on the table, and she would swat at Justice if he did. But here she was, with her elbows on the table and her head in her hands.

At last, he heard her voice. Words. She was finally speaking to him. He felt a huge wave of relief, even though he was pretty sure he didn't want to hear what she had to say. She was rubbing her forehead as if she had a splitting headache.

"What in the world would make you do something like this, Justice? You, of all people? A common thief? Why did you steal your teacher's phone and wallet?"

"Ma…!"

"That was who was on the phone. Ms. Clarendon. A nice woman. So, OK, you returned the cellphone. She was happy about that. But what about the wallet?"

"Ma…!"

"Where is that? What did you do with it?"

"Ma…!"

"I can't believe I'm having this conversation with you, Justice. This isn't you. This isn't the boy I raised."

Justice tried to break in. But he kept getting knocked back out of the conversation by his mother's fury. By her disappointment in him. But when she finally paused to catch her breath, he didn't take his chance to jump in. He was distracted by something she had said. Ms. C's cell phone. It had been returned.

Maybe Ebony isn't so bad, after all. Maybe she was sorry. But why didn't she return the wallet too?

His mother interrupted his train of thought. She had caught her breath and was winding up for another round of attack.

"Uh, hello! Excuse me, Jay! Don't you hear me talking to you? What is wrong with you? I just can't believe this! Why would you embarrass me like this? Why would you embarrass yourself? I told her that I needed to talk to you and then I would call her back. I know there has to be something more to this whole situation. I know my son isn't a thief because I know I raised you better than that. So come on now, tell me what's going on."

Even though she was yelling at him, Justice was relieved that she was at least talking to him. He could tell the worst of her anger was already passing. She was asking him questions now. She was ready to listen to him. Ready to believe what he had to say. Ready to believe in her son again.

Justice didn't even stop to think about what he wanted to say. Which words to choose. How he could make himself look better here. He just dove right in, and the words came pouring out.

"There's this girl, Ebony, in my class. Ma, she's so beautiful. And she's smart and sweet and kind. I won't lie—I have a huge crush on her…"

Justice began there and quickly told his mother everything, from beginning to end. The F on his English test. The make-up test. His rapping those lyrics that bothered Ms. C. His joking with her about her purse and how easy it would be to rob her. What he saw Ebony do. How he tried to talk to her afterwards. His run-in with Mr. Hencken and Ms. C in the hallway.

"I like this girl so much, Ma. I can't snitch on her. I'd rather take the blame myself. And I still think she didn't do it. Or, I guess she did, but there's something else going on here. She wouldn't dream of doing something like this. Not without a good reason. I'm sure of it."

"Well, I hope you're right, Justice. I don't like the idea of you falling head over heels for someone who steals stuff. Steals right out of another woman's purse. A teacher's purse. One of the nicest and fairest teachers in the school. One who actually cares about her students and tries to help them make something of themselves."

Justice's mother paused. Her brow wrinkled in thought.

"But...I agree with you. Something doesn't add up here. If what you say about Ebony is true, she is acting out of character. There must be something wrong. Something that would make her do this crazy thing."

She paused again.

"I do trust you, Justice. And I believe you. And I think you're right about Ebony. You've always been a good judge of character. You make good friends. You choose good people to hang out with."

Justice's mother's eyes filled with tears. She reached for his hand.

"I hope you know how much I cherish our relationship. I am so grateful that you feel comfortable enough to talk to me and tell me what's on your mind and in your heart. A lot of mothers aren't that lucky. And they're always in the dark and worried about their kids. You know you can always come to me with any problems. You can tell me anything. And we'll always figure it out together. You know this, right?"

"Aw yeah, Ma. I know that."

Justice squeezed her hand and kissed her on the cheek. They both smiled at each other. Soon, his mother's smile faded. She had a serious expression on her face again.

"Now, Justice. I admire you for wanting to take the blame for Ebony. But I can't allow you to do that. You're innocent and you can't take the fall for someone else's mistake. No matter what your feelings for her or what is going on in her life, Ebony has to take responsibility for this. She has to own up to it. Face the music. Accept the consequences."

"I know that now, Ma. I understand."

"Which doesn't mean you can't help her through it. We both can."

"How, Ma?"

"I think I have an idea. Excuse me for a moment, Justice. I have a phone call to make."

CHAPTER 8

"Hurry up, Justice! Your breakfast is ready. Come on, you'll make us late!"

"COMING!"

Justice had awoken from a deep, dreamless sleep. He had been so worn out from the events of the day. When his head hit the pillow last night, he was practically snoring already. He slept so much better than the previous night. But now his mom was yelling for him to get up and out. All that had happened over the last two days came flooding back. All the worry and stress and disappointment and bad feelings. And today might not be much better. There were going to be some tough conversations. Some uncomfortable encounters.

"Breakfast is ready, Justice. Shake a leg!"

Let me guess. Dry toast, a hardboiled egg, and fried bologna. The usual. Breakfast of champions.

Justice left his room and walked to the dining table. It wasn't the usual. Not at all. Blueberry pancakes and syrup, scrambled eggs with cheese, sausages. Even some shredded and fried potatoes!

"What a feast! What's the occasion, Ma?"

"No special occasion. Nothing but the best for the best son in the world."

Justice smiled shyly.

"And we're going to need some energy and brain food this morning. Right, Justice?"

"You got that right," Justice replied, sighing a little.

"Don't worry, baby. This is all going to work out fine. You'll see. I promise."

Last night, his mother had called Ms. Clarendon. She filled Justice in on the phone conversation right before bed. Somehow his mother had managed to explain the misunderstanding to Ms. C and convince her of Justice's innocence.

"He was trying so hard to do the right thing, Ms. Clarendon. For everyone involved."

Justice's mom told him everything Ms. C had said and done. After his mom had finished explaining the situation, Ms. C was silent for a long time. Then she cleared her throat. She began to speak but quickly stopped. Her voice sort of gave out. She cleared her throat and tried again. Ms. C said she believed what Justice's mother had told her. Justice's mother then asked her to meet with herself, Justice, Ebony, and Ebony's mother the next morning at school. To get it all out in the open. To sort and straighten it all out. To deal with it.

"Yes, I think that's a good idea. I have some things I'd like to say to Justice. I'll contact Ebony's mother right now and set it up."

And that was how his mom's conversation with Ms. C had ended.

"So there's nothing to worry about anymore, Justice," his mother again reassured him over breakfast. "Today is a brand new day, and it's going to be a really good one. I can just feel it."

Justice looked at his mother with awe and thanks. And with love. She was a miracle worker. A superhero. His mother had saved the day.

"I love you, Ma."

"I love you too, baby. Now hurry up and get eating. We don't want to be late. Not this morning."

Justice and his mother arrived early. Ebony and her mother had gotten there even earlier. They were already waiting in the office when Justice and his mother walked in.

Well, here we go.

Justice took a deep breath and tried to steady his nerves. Justice glanced at Ebony shyly. A little guiltily. Quietly, he said, "Hey, Ebony."

"Hey," Ebony responded. She didn't meet his eyes but kept staring straight ahead.

Is she mad at me? Embarrassed? Nervous? All of the above?

Ebony's mother was the first Japanese woman Justice had ever met. There were some

Chinese and Koreans in the 'hood, but there were no Japanese. She was just as beautiful as Ebony.

Justice's mom extended her hand to Ebony's mother.

"I'm Ericka Alexander, Justice's mother. Pleased to meet you."

"My name is Shinobu Aikyo. I am very honored to meet you. Ebony speaks very highly of your son." Her words were careful and slow.

She does?! Well, maybe she used to. Probably not anymore, Justice thought miserably.

"And my son is a huge fan of Ebony's."

Watch it, Ma. Go easy. Don't embarrass me worse than I already am.

Their mothers were hitting it off.

What a relief!

The atmosphere in the room relaxed. Everyone exhaled. Maybe it was all going to be OK after all. Justice snuck a peek at Ebony. Even she looked a little less tense than a few minutes ago. Justice tried to act casual and easy as he chose a seat right next to her and lowered himself into it.

While their mothers were getting to know each other, Justice whispered to Ebony, "For real, I didn't snitch to Ms. C or Mr. Hencken. I swear to you, Ebony. Ms. C called my mom and told her that I stole her phone and wallet. My mother was heartbroken. And it looked like she wanted to kill me. So I had to come clean. But I think everything's going to be OK. I really do."

Ebony was about to respond when Ms. C arrived and asked them all to join her in her classroom. Whatever Ebony had to say to Justice would have to wait. Justice was in agony, wondering if their friendship or romance—or whatever it might be—was over. Just like that. Before it had even really begun.

Once they had all entered the classroom, Ms. C said, "Thank you for taking the time out of your busy day to meet with me this morning. Please, everyone, take a seat."

The seats were arranged in a circle. Ms. C thought this was the best way for everyone to be seen and heard. It put everyone on an equal footing.

They had barely sat down and settled in

when Ebony caught everyone off guard by suddenly blurting out, "I'm sorry, Miss Clarendon! I'm so sorry I took your things from your bag. I have never done anything like that before. I'm so embarrassed. I don't know what made me do something like that. I know it wasn't right, but I'm just so tired of..."

Ebony stopped in the middle of her sentence. She looked over at her mother, then dropped her head. Tears began streaming down her face, and her body was shaking with sobs. The fact that she was crying made Justice slightly uncomfortable. He wanted to do something—hold her hand, hug her, wipe her tears away—but there was nothing he could do. Not here, not now. So instead, he simply pulled his chair closer to hers, hoping this would comfort her just a little.

Ms. Clarendon leaned over and put her hand on Ebony's knee.

"It's OK, Ebony. I accept your apology. OK, sweetheart? Everything is going to be just fine. That's why we're all here now. So we can work things out, alright?

"No, Ms. C, you don't understand. I mean,

I am upset for taking your stuff. Straight up. But it's not just that. It's...I'm so tired...so tired of...I just wanted something good... something nice...for myself..."

Ebony again glanced at her mother. Ms. Aikyo began to speak. But after opening her mouth, she hesitated. Stopped. A few long seconds passed. She took a deep, shaky breath and began again, slowly. Carefully.

"I am so sorry. English is not my first language. But please...take this."

She handed Ms. C her wallet back.

"I am sorry. Ebony is sorry too. Very sorry. I will pay you back, OK? I will pay you back. As soon as I find a job. I look for work every day. One day soon, I will find a job. And I will pay you back, OK?"

Ms. Aikyo looked at Ebony. Her daughter was crying even more now. A flash of pain crossed Ms. Aikyo's face.

"I do not want to hurt you, Ebony, but I have to tell your teacher what has been going on. Ebony does not want anyone to know that we sleep in our car. We go to Starbucks every morning to wash. We have nowhere to go. Nowhere to live. There is no father, no husband, anymore. I will find work. I know I will. I will pay you back, OK? I will pay!"

Wait! What is she saying? Ebony and her mother are...homeless?!

CHAPTER 9

So that's why I could never figure out where Ebony lived! Ebony is...homeless. Justice's heart was breaking for her.

Justice could tell Ms. Clarendon was also surprised by the news that Ebony and her mother were homeless. She always prided herself on knowing her students. On really seeing them and their lives and their struggles. She had been totally blind. She never suspected Ebony was facing these challenges. How could she? Ebony was a star student and always so well put together.

How did she manage both of these things while living out of a car?!

Justice's mother seemed to be reading Ms. C's mind. She spoke up.

"I just can't imagine how you have survived on the streets this long without getting into any serious trouble. And you both look so great. And Ebony, you are doing so well at school. You two are amazing! But I can't see you living out of that car another night. Justice and I don't have much, but you can stay with us for the time being."

Ms. Aikyo began to object.

"No, we can not accept. We would be too much trouble..."

"You WILL stay with us, just until we figure something else out," Justice's mom insisted. "Maybe I can see if the company I work for can help out in some way. My boss is a real nice man. He must need some extra help around the office."

Ms. Clarendon cut in. "First of all, as far as the wallet and the money...we're forgetting about all that. That is done and past. Let's focus on what we can do to get you a permanent place to live and a decent job. Ms. Alexander, it would be great if you could ask your boss about any open positions. And it is so nice of you to offer Ms. Aikyo a place to stay for a few days, but I am going to make sure they have some place to stay before I leave here today, OK? Ms. Aikyo, can you come see me again after school today? By then I will have found a placement for you at a decent women's shelter near by. That will be just temporary. Just until we can find you an apartment of your own."

"I see now why Ms. Clarendon is your favorite teacher, Justice," his mom said to him.

Justice smiled and nodded. Ms. C went above and beyond the call of duty to help her students. She was a wonderful person, even if she did occasionally make mistakes and snap judgments. Who didn't?

"OK, Ms. Clarendon," said Justice's mom. "But just let me know if you can't arrange things with the shelter. My home is their home, for as long as necessary. And I will check in with my boss. The other day I heard somebody saying something about a position in the mailroom opening up."

Ebony's mother had tears in her eyes. In

a trembling voice, she said, "Thank you so much for your kindness, Ms. Clarendon, Ms. Alexander." She clasped her hands together in thanks and bowed her head several times. She was too choked up to say more.

Instead of shaking hands as their meeting broke up, Ms. Clarendon suggested a group hug. While they were all locked in a tight embrace, Ms. Clarendon announced, "OK, there is one more thing I'd like to add." She looked at Justice with a sad and serious expression.

"Justice, I am so sorry that I accused you of taking my things without any evidence to support it. All I really had was just a lot of prejudiced ideas about who you are and how some people may see you or what they think of you. It was just a really stupid thing to do on my part. I feel like such an idiot. I always thought I was better and smarter than that. I am so disappointed in myself. You are truly an amazing young man. I mean, just look what you've done here, bringing us all together and helping people out. And I am really sorry. I hope you can accept my apology. I hope you can forgive me and trust me again."

Justice was blown away. No teacher had ever spoken to him like that before. No authority figure. Especially not a white person.

Ms. C was wrong. She knows me pretty well, but at the first hint of trouble, she saw a white person's version of a young black man. She wasn't seeing me anymore. She wasn't seeing Justice. Just like my mom was trying to tell me the other morning. She warned me. She was right. Ms. C was wrong.

But she is apologizing. And she really means it, I can tell. She feels terrible. I need to really see her right now. See Ms. Clarendon. Not just some mean teacher, some mean white lady. Because that's not who she really is. I need to see her clearly, flaws and all. She's a good person. She cares about us. She works hard to help us. She's trying. And she doesn't have to. Not really. But she's here every day, trying. That's what is important. That's Ms. C.

"It's cool, Ms. C. I accept your apology. It's all right. We all make mistakes. We all get people wrong sometimes."

He looked over at his mother and smiled.

"We learn something new every day, right? We're all just teaching each other."

Justice's mom and Ms. Aikyo left the building together, chatting away as if they were old friends. Justice reached for Ebony's hand.

"I'll see you later, alright?"

He made her blush.

"OK, see you later. And Justice? Thank you."

For the rest of the day, between periods, at lunch, after school, Justice and Ebony were inseparable. Eric saw them sitting together in the cafeteria and in between classes. When he saw Ebony take a seat next to Justice in Ms. Clarendon's class, he leaned over and said, "That's my boy. I see you. Way to step yo' game up, bro. That's what I'm talking 'bout!"

Justice looked at Ebony, but thankfully she wasn't paying any attention. He blushed. Eric said, "Uh-oh, looks like I'm dealing with Mr. Romeo. You might be giving up your player card, man."

"Whatever, yo. You crazy, man."

"Naw, you crazy. Crazy in love."

They laughed. Justice was feeling really good today. It had been a great day. So much better than he had expected. He sat up in his chair and opened his textbook. He glanced over at Ebony. And for the first time, he admitted it to himself. It was true. Eric was right, for once.

Justice was falling in love.

WANT TO KEEP READING?

If you liked this book, check out another book
from West 44 Books:

DREAMS ON FIRE
BY ANNETTE DANIELS TAYLOR

ISBN: 9781538382479

Home Filled with Sounds of Music

Every day,
every night.
Daddy wrote love songs.
Mama would sing them
just right.
Every rehearsal she'd sing
romantic melodies
of how perfect love could be.

One night
inside Pandora's Box,
a drunk put his hand on Mama.

Daddy kicked him out.
The band laughed.
Some drinks were drunk.
Rehearsal began again.

The door opened.
That man came back,
looking through
bloodshot eyes.

Threatening Daddy
with his gun.
Threatening Daddy
to end his life.

Folks dove.
To the floor they fled.
A practiced safety routine.

That man didn't know…

Daddy Carried a Gun

That's why that man is dead.

Lawyer:	*Self-defense!*
District Attorney:	*Concealed weapon. Murder, second degree!*
Daddy:	*Pick up your heads!*
Grandma:	*Pray up to the begotten Son.*
Mama:	*Hurting, need to forget…*

Daddy in prison.
Judge gave 25 years.
Good behavior lessens time,
not Mama's tears.

Dreams on **FIRE**

Annette Daniels Taylor

The Same **Blood**

M. AZMITIA

FIFTEEN AND CHANGE

BY MAX HOWARD

SECOND IN COMMAND

Sandi Van

Check out more books at:
www.west44books.com

An imprint of Enslow Publishing

WEST **44** BOOKS™